Make each day a
New Adventure!

♡ Cherish
+
-Dr. Benjamin Hummez

What Would You Like To Do Today?

Larry Grizzell

Illustrated by Cherish Flieder & Benjamin Hummel

ADVENTURES GALORE · LAKE GEORGE, COLORADO

Request for permission to make copies of any part of
the work should be mailed to the following address:
ACL, P.O. Box 748, Lake George, CO 80827.

www.adventuresgalore.com

Library of Congress Control Number 2004096579

Summary: What Would You Like To Do Today?
Simple adventures of childhood pleasures.
[1. Children's activities - Non-Fiction
2. Children's adventures - Non-Fiction]

ISBN 0975954202

Published in the United States of America
Print Executors
Citicap Channels Ltd, New Delhi, India
www.citibazaar.com / connect@citibazaar.com

The artwork was executed in watercolor, colored pencil,
pastels and oil on 300 lb. cold press Arches watercolor paper.
The text is Goudy Old Style.
The book layout and design was completed by
Cherished Solutions, llc., Golden, Colorado.
www.cherishedsolutions.com

Here's what others have to say about
What Would You Like To Do Today!

"As a mother of two boys, this book really hit home with me.
I am constantly trying to find new, exciting things to do to
entertain them. This book has helped me and my children
see that doing simple things can be fun and rewarding."

–René Dabbs, mom and former Marketing Manager, Focus On The Family.

"Not only is this book a great legacy for [the author's]
own grandchildren, but it is a beautiful gift to
all who enjoy good children's literature."

–Mrs. Ruth J. Scott, primary teacher.

"This gorgeous book is about the simple
adventures of childhood and the importance
of everyday pleasures. With today's hurry-
up attitudes and jam-packed schedules, it
reminds us to slow down and enjoy the day.
I recommend it to everyone with young
children or grandchildren."

–Dee Mills, author, teacher and mother.

This book is dedicated:

This Book Belongs To:

_____

A Loving Gift From:

_____

On This Special Day:

_____

What would you like to do today?
After we take the time to pray,
maybe we could go outside and play.

Maybe you would like to ride your bike,

or we could take a nice long hike.

We could stay inside and read a book,

or walk along a babbling brook.

How about if we baked a cake,

or skipped some stones across the lake?

What if we just took a walk,
and found a cozy place to talk?

You and I
could play leap frog,
and then we could
wrestle with the dog.

What would you like to do today?
The choice is yours,
whatever you say!
We could play tag or hide-n-seek.
You hide first, I won't peek.

You could build a castle in the sand,
or pretend you're in a marching band.

Would you enjoy a piggy-back ride,
or maybe you'd rather go down a slide?

What would you like to do today? I'm ready when you are.

Let's go play!

Appendix: Ideas and Suggestions

Most of these ideas have been passed on to me by friends and relatives:

- Try asking your children this question: "How would you like to go on an adventure next Saturday?" Wait for a response. More than likely they will answer, "What are we going to do?" If you have something in mind, tell them. I've found it more suspenseful to tell them it's going to be a surprise. It's amazing how calling something an adventure gets people excited. I can call cleaning the barn an adventure and my grandchildren will pitch right in. Seriously, it never gets old, and almost everything we do is an adventure.

- We all know that children are constantly asking to do things, go somewhere, or buy something. This next idea will work almost every time: Keep a list of planned adventures. In other words, whenever the child asks for anything, agree to write it down, or if they are old enough, let them write it down. I keep on my desk a list of adventures for my grandchildren that we can check off when completed. That sure beats the standard answer, "I'll think about it," that most children receive. In fact, I carry a small voice recorder (*Voice It*) everywhere I go, and now they just say, "Grandpa, put it on your *Voice It*!"

- While rearing our three sons, who were each three years apart, we found it challenging to do things that were of interest to all of them. This idea worked well for us most of the time: Each son would write down some fun things he wanted to do, or places he wanted to go on separate pieces of paper. All of the pieces were then collected and placed in a jar. My wife, without looking, would then reach into the jar and select a piece of paper. Very slowly and with great dramatic fanfare, she would announce our next adventure. Everybody wins!

- This next suggestion works wonders with children of all ages. Be careful using this idea . . . someone might think you've lost it! Once a week, give someone in the family a surprise gift, something inexpensive at a time they least expect it. Children observing adults practicing this "love gift" activity learn a valuable lesson. Of course, include the children in the gift giving as well. Next, once a week, give someone you love a surprise hug for no reason at all, at a time they least expect it. Children observing adults hugging receive just as meaningful a lesson as when they are hugged themselves. Finally, once a week (at least) pay a sincere compliment to a complete stranger when they least expect it. Do this as often as possible in front of children and they will soon understand. We all know that living examples are the best way for children to learn, and these three adventures in giving are powerful principles.

Thank you for purchasing this book. You may order a gift copy at our web site and have it inscribed and sent anywhere in the United States or Canada. For additional gift ideas and fun things to do, visit us at www.AdventuresGalore.com. I welcome your comments. You can reach me at info@adventuresgalore.com. Now, *What Would You Like To Do Today?*

—Larry Grizzell